To: The O'Brien's

Keep Reading
+ Wear Your Helmet

MY TIME ON NANTUCKET

by
Chuckie Veneziano
Illus. by Stan Jaskiel

©2004 by Chuck Veneziano
Published by Sweet Punkin Press,
P.O. Box 405, Medford, MA 02155-4605

ISBN 0-9755078-0-X
Library Of Congress 2004093577
First Edition 10 9 8 7 6 5 4 3 2
Printed in Massachusetts USA

ACK –nowledgements:

*ACK is the identifier for the Nantucket Airport

Special thanks to: **Gloria**, my Mom, for your love and support..

Andrew, Christian & Ariana, my niece and nephews, for helping me see things through a child's eye.

Stan Jaskiel, my illustrator for bringing my story to life. I appreciate your patience.

Hank Morse for your support and advice.

Vinnie Tirone for your help in all stages of this book.

Laura Dalessio Baccini for bringing this book through it's final stages and trusting it's potential.

Medford Kiwanis & Chamber of Commerce

Frank Interrante

Victor & Lyn DiMare

Lisa (Forz) & Jim Ferraguto, Lisa DiRocco

The Gentile's, The Baccini's

My Brothers; Domenic, Ricky & John

Robert, Grandma, Patty & Debbie

Cheryl Zagami, Punkin, Sweet Pea, Cisco & Fred

Laura Olifer (1.3)

Christine Callahan, Andrea Cangiano, Nancy & Scott Morrissey, Joey & Christine Joyce,

Joe & Tracy Mahoney, Rich & Tracy Zampitella, Gordan & Christine Maloney, G.J. & Karen Bradanese

Mark Matarazzo & Michelle, Gerry Celano & Kelly, Lainie Silva, Linda Dalessio, Ellie Brady, Lee Viola, Annie DeWolfe,

Author Fran Hodgkin, Nancy & Thayer McCain, Kathy Cali, Audrey & Tom Killion

Two Johanson, Mike & Wendy Murphy, Andrea Giacalone

Andrew & Christine Curtin, Lucia Vanaria, Dave Cruz, Anna, Mat, Ed, Brian, Paul

For the many, many others who helped me along the way, including but not limited to the names printed in the island. Thanks so much!

Dedication

We all believe we have so much time on earth,
until we hit a certain age and ask where all that time went.
My Dad was only 69 when his time was cut short, losing a battle to cancer.
His passing, though sad, was the motivational factor that helped take this book to completion.
I dedicate this book to his life. He was a good father, coach and friend.

My hope is that this dedication will inspire others to take a chance in life
and share what they have written .
Life is way to short for procrastination and hiding things in a drawer for another day.
If you've hit that certain age when you're asking _that_ question,
Then you know exactly what I'm talking about.

"There is nothing sadder than wasted talent;" a line I remember from "A Bronx Tale".
Many of us have people that we miss in the worst way, as in the case with my Dad.
Let their passing remind us how important today really is,
for no one is ever promised a tomorrow.

It began on a ship headed straight out to sea,
with my mother, my father, my sister and me.

To the island of *Nantucket* we were headed that day,
for biking, beaches and to just get away.

My parents were reading, my sister she wrote;
but I had a big job... I captained the boat!

And I was determined to get us there fast
so I pushed on the throttle and gave it some gas.

Oh, what a thrill being out at sea,
and to have all those people depending on me,

to warn off ships if they get too near,
and to get us safely to *Nantucket's* pier.

When we docked at the island,
I passed the captain's hat to Dawn,
a pretty young lady, who was just getting on.

Then I walked off the boat onto a cobblestone street.
My parents were hungry so we all went to eat.

We each ordered something and when it was ready, out came my meatballs and plate of spaghetti.

My Mom had chicken, my Dad had fish and my sister had a little from everyone's dish.

After lunch we went back to the street.
I looked all around and thought, "Wow, this is neat!"

There were little gray houses with things for sale
and a place I noticed to go watch a whale.

They had windsurfers and fishing gear to buy or to rent,
and bicycle shops... Yup... that's where we went.

I picked out a red bike, my Mom's bike was black, and my Dad got a blue one with a seat on the back.

Then we each got a helmet to wear on our head, "Safety comes first" is what Mom always said.

It was getting late now and it was time to check in.
We had two rooms reserved at The Stumble Inn.

There was an Innkeeper there named Suzie Magee.
A kind old lady with a badly bruised knee.

I said, "Excuse me Suzie, but what did you do
that gave you such a bad boo-boo?
Did it hurt a lot? Did it make you cry?"
then I stood there eager for her reply.

She said, "See those flowers yellow and red,
lying in that flower bed?

I did all that work three days ago,
creating that beautiful sight.

But when I was done, I put nothing away and
fell over my tools one night.

So let that be a lesson children, anytime you play,
when you're done having fun, put all your things away."

I smiled at her and thanked her for the advice,
and whispered to my parents that I thought she was nice.

Then with no one asking and without a peep,
my sister and I fell fast asleep.

The next day I was up at dawn
and I rushed to put my bathing suit on.

I grabbed my shovel and pail and did not cry
when my mother put sun block on my sister and I.

Then we gathered our things with no big fuss
and went out to catch the shuttle bus.

The beach was *Jetties*, a family beach.
From town it was the easiest beach to reach.

There's a bath house and a playground too
and lifeguards to keep an eye on you.

From 9:00 to 3:00 we had so much fun,
swimming and splashing under the warmth of the sun.

Flying our kites high in the sky,
making sand castles and eating french fries.

In fact, before we knew it, the whole day was through.
We ate dinner, watched TV and dreamt of day two.

With the next day here we got our bikes off the rack,
put our helmets in place and grabbed our backpacks.

We tried riding through town but what a sensation!
The cobblestone streets caused an awful vibration!

So we walked to the bike path and cycled away.
We saw so many wonderful things that day!

Like the *Old Mill* on the hill that still grinds corn,
and *The Hadwen House* built before we were born.

The *Old Gaol* where the bad guys were kept
and the *Greater Light Home* where Quaker sisters slept.

Old Gaol

Hadwen House

Old Mill

We had people wave to us as they lay on their lawn, relaxing with their sunglasses on.

And rollerbladers trying to match our pace, huffing and puffing till they were red in the face!

We saw birds fly by like they were in some big rush
and bunnies scatter into very thick brush.

We saw so many things like I said before,
but I have to tell you about just one more.

We all got off our bikes at *Hammond Pond* dock,
and set them down gently on the side of a rock.

The Innkeeper, Suzie Magee, was there with something
she said she was hoping to share.

"When I was your age, someone showed this to me.
I never forgot it, now I'd like you to see."

And without another word, she began her thing.
She took a raw piece of chicken and a handful of string.

Then she tied them together in a cute little bow
and lowered it to the water e-x-t-r-e-m-e-l-y slow.

We all waited a minute, then two, then three,
when all of a sudden looking right back at me,

were two little eyes, then a nose, then a face.
The nose blew water all over the place!

No one moved a muscle. No one turned around.
We just stared at the water without making a sound.

We saw his eyes roll left, then to the right.
Then he spotted the chicken and when the time was right,

he reached with his legs, stuck out his claws,
and bit down hard with powerful jaws.

And just as he did, Suzie pulled on the string,
lifted the chicken and lifted this thing!

"What is it Suzie? What is it?" I cried.
"It's a snapping turtle" Suzie replied.

"A snapping turtle, like the one I once saw,
with a hard shell on its back, a powerful jaw,
four thick legs and I tell you my friend,
it even has a tail at the end!"

"So take a good look everybody", Suzie said with a glow,
"Because in a very short time, I must untie this bow.

So that the snapping turtle can go home once again
and share his feast with family and friends."

When the bow was untied, the turtle vanished from sight,
and like all of us, he went home for the night.

Later that evening as I lay awake in bed
reliving the last two days in my head

I thought of my sister, my Mom and my Dad,
and the weekend of fun that we all had.

And I thought of the innkeeper, Suzie Magee
today at the pond and all the lessons she taught me.

And I thought of *Nantucket*, though small in size,
so full of excitement and full of surprise!

And I fell sound asleep with a smile on my face,
thanks to my time on *Nantucket*,
what a wonderful, wonderful place.

My Time On Nantucket is a product of Sweet Punkin Press

Where a good rhyme is a good read.™

Quick Order Form

Fax Orders: 978-663-7563. Send copy of form.
Email Orders: sweetpunkinpress@aol.com
Postal Orders: Sweet Punkin Press, 43 Riverside Avenue #405, Medford, MA 02155
Website: www.SweetPunkinPress.com

Name: _____
Address:_____

City: _____ State: _____ Zip: _____
Telephone: _____ Cell: _____
Email Address: _____

[ ] My Time On Nantucket, hardcover book $17.95
[ ] My Time On Nantucket Coloring Book $ 3.95
[ ] My Time On Nantucket CD $11.95
[ ] My Time On Nantucket Special Package $24.95
    (package includes all three at a savings of $5.00)

Shipping, U.S.: $4.00 for first book, CD or package and $2.00 for each additional product.
Payment: [ ] Check [ ] Credit Card: [ ] VISA [ ] MasterCard [ ] American Express [ ] Discover
Card Number: _____
Name on card: _____ Exp. Date: _____